PORTRAIT

·OF A·

FATHER

ROBERT PENN

W·A·R·R·E·N

PORTRAIT
OF A
F·A·T·H·E·R

THE UNIVERSITY PRESS OF KENTUCKY

Publication of this book has been assisted
by a grant from the Gannett Foundation

Published by the University Press of Kentucky

Scholarly publisher for the Commonwealth,
serving Bellarmine College, Berea College, Centre
College of Kentucky, Eastern Kentucky University,
The Filson Club, Georgetown College, Kentucky
Historical Society, Kentucky State University,
Morehead State University, Murray State University,
Northern Kentucky University, Transylvania University,
University of Kentucky, University of Louisville,
and Western Kentucky University.

Editorial and Sales Offices: Lexington, Kentucky 40506-0336

The essay "Portrait of a Father" was originally published in *The Southern
Review* (Spring 1987). "Mortmain," copyright 1960 by Robert Penn Warren,
is from *New and Selected Poems, 1923-1985* by Robert Penn Warren,
published by Random House, Inc. Both "Portrait of a Father" and
"Mortmain" have been revised by the author for this edition.

Library of Congress Cataloging-in-Publication
Data appear at the end of the book.

PORTRAIT
·OF A·
FATHER

MY FATHER, as the years since his death pass, becomes to me more and more a man of mystery. I do not mean to say that I do not know the man he was. The personality and character of no man could be more clearly delineated—and this in even the smallest detail. What is mysterious is the personal history from which that man emerged. This involves, of course, the mystery of his family, especially of his mother and father.

Here I must mention another mystery, a related mystery which, strangely enough until now, I had not recognized as a mystery. My mother, who had told me much of the past, had never, not even once, mentioned her earlier acquaintance with the man whom she was to marry. Certainly, he was not at that time living in the region, nor had been there when her family came. As far as her account went, her husband might not have even existed until her wedding day in 1904.

Once when I was a boy, I saw, very briefly, in the hands of my grandfather's second wife, what I then supposed to be the Bible of my father's family. In any case, it presumably had the date of my father's birth written inside. But, long since, I have decided that it must have been a new Bible bought after her marriage to become her own family Bible. If so, she had chosen the right stepson to claim for her record. After the death of her husband that stepson, though he could at that time ill afford it, bought her a house and watched over her, even if he rarely saw her.

I knew "Grandma Jenny" because every summer of my boyhood I spent long periods with my maternal grandfather on his farm, a few miles away from her house in the village of Cerulean Springs, Kentucky. Once a year I was to make her the visit of a day and a night. This was at my father's command, for, as a boy, I found that visit dull, especially with her dull daughter and son-in-law. My father stood his ground and stated that his stepmother was a "good" woman who did "the best she could according to the lights available to her." Indeed such a phrase was not uncommon on his lips: according to the "lights available" to the person in question.

All that I know of my paternal grandfather is that he,

a captain I seem to remember, had served in the Confederate army, and had fought first at Shiloh—where my maternal grandfather had found his own first baptism of fire. That was all that my father ever told me of his family except that the first Warren of his family had come to Virginia "fairly early," and that his people, toward the War of 1812, had pioneered from North Carolina, across Tennessee, to the Valley of the Cumberland in the southwest of Kentucky.

I must now speak of my father as I remember him from my boyhood. At that time, he was six feet tall. I know this because, when I was a boy of fifteen or so and was worried about my own slow growth, I asked him how tall he was. At another time he told me that he had never weighed more than one hundred and forty-five pounds. He looked much larger because his shoulders were broad and he was, even into some years, very erect. He was, as I knew from a boy's curiosity and observation, unusually strong. I had early noticed that his body seemed to be all bone and sinew.

His features were regular but with a somewhat prominent Roman nose. His eyes were a kind of brownish-hazel color. His ordinary expression was calm, but sometimes thoughtful and even introspective. The jaws seemed to be carried firmly but unaggressively. In usual greeting or in pleasure his smile might be sudden, and occasionally, infectious.

My father's health—or it may often have been only self-control—was remarkable. Never in his eighty-five years was he to spend a day in bed or even see a doctor except during one protracted illness when I was six years old. In his entire life he never went to a dentist. Shortly before his death he remarked: "Naturally, in late years, I have had to remove two or three teeth myself." It must be added that if wife or child had even a hurt finger a doctor was called. No theology had ever been involved in the issue.

At one time he told me that when he was twenty-nine he had been going "seriously" bald. Hair, he said, was coming out by the "handful." In saying this he had made a sudden unconscious gesture, up and down, with his right hand, as though throwing something to the floor— as though repeating an angry or despairing gesture from all those years before. For that instant there was the angry and despairing expression on his face which I had never seen before, nor have ever seen since. At that period he had been courting a girl some years younger than he. Her name was Anna Ruth Penn.

Bald or not, he was successful in his suit. Year after year, on his birthday, February 14, when at breakfast time my mother would pass behind his chair, she would lean in her humorous and loving way and kiss the top of the bald pate and murmur: "My comic valentine." He would blush and stir in a kind of boyish embarrassment, and say: "Oh, shucks."

Later on, when such things might cross my mind, I imagined that he must have been a rather handsome young man. Even as I now think of him in his forties he was somewhat memorable, with the dignified calm of his face, the thrust of his Roman nose, and, especially in the glint of artificial light, the bald head seeming to be carved from some stone, even marble. Not that in my boyhood I had ever seen a bust, or any statuary, except in pictures. Certainly there had been some such pictures in the books of history which he had begun very often to read to me.

For another preliminary but to me important general fact, there was his positive aversion to violence of any kind. This fact seemed then a trifle more odd than now. Personal violence seemed, by hearsay at least, common and even in principle acceptable. A neighbor of ours was generally known to have shot a man to death. He was a citizen in good standing. My father never mentioned

11

this matter to me, and more than once as I grew older he said that law is "the mark of civilization."

Certainly he could know anger, and I recognized the physical signals of that rare anger: a widening of the nostrils and a whitening of the flanges toward the base, and a tightening of the muscles of the jaw on each side so that the muscles would bulge a little. His words would then be much slower than usual, carefully spaced, seemingly very impersonal. Indeed, the anger usually seemed to be somehow directed to a general attitude or idea rather than to a person who might be involved.

Strangely enough with all his aversion to violence, my father remarked more than once over the years of my childhood that anyone who broke into and entered a dwelling, or came by stealth, was a potential murderer and that on a jury he would never vote guilty against a householder who had shot such an intruder dead.

Only once did I ever see him in a violent action. When I was a child, once in the middle of the night, I heard a racket from the bedroom of our parents, and ran there. There, in his gray flannel nightshirt, my father stood, the two bony big toes curling up from the cold floor. This trivial detail stuck in my mind for good, almost as emphatically as the fact that with both hands he held a heavy iron bar. He was breathing hard, with a kind of glitter on his face. I saw it all because I had just switched on the light.

By his account he had come awake at some small and not repeated sound. Then by the light of last coals in the grate he had seen moving the knob of the door to the bathroom on the far side of the bed, where our mother was sleeping. Slowly, bit by bit, the knob was turning. He slipped from bed, saw the bar, still half-wrapped, propped in a corner. He silently seized it. The bar, an odd object for a bedroom, he had bought that afternoon and brought home to be used in the coal house to break big chunks.

The door from the bathroom would open into the bedroom, and so he took position to the hinged side. He waited with the bar raised. A head was slowly coming through the space. He later said that his blow was premature, that he should have waited another second or two. The bar struck a slightly glancing blow against the edge of the door, but with such solid force that it came down on the slowly emerging head. It must have been the yell that woke me up.

After the first stroke the intruder fell back into the bathtub. My father, a very careful man, said that he had withheld a second stroke so as not to ruin the bathtub. He said that he had intended to "mow" the man down as the head lifted above the edge of the tub. He did get in another stroke, but somehow the victim managed to keep rising and dove through the window of the bathroom. It was a first-floor window.

In any case, the next morning there was blood spattered on the snow. Or was there snow? My father, standing with the bar grasped in both hands, asserted that if he had only had shoes on he would have followed the man and "fixed him." There still was, as has been noted, a sort of "glitter" on his face. Many years later I have wondered—merely wondered—if his abhorrence of all violence may have been directed inwardly.

As a sort of appendix to my father's one scene of violence, I vaguely recall some remark in town that the "intruder" had probably been some "stray nigger." My father had never commented on the race of his victim. I remember very distinctly the moment later on when one of the children (I may have been the child) used at home a word possibly picked up on the school playground: *nigger*. My father very slowly and objectively said: "That word will never be used in this house." It never again was.

Some years later he remarked, this time factually and

not in rebuke, that he had rarely known a man of any color who "if you treated him right, wouldn't try to treat you right." My father was never acting as any sort of crusader. He merely had his view of the world. It was no secret.

In tiny casual scraps I picked up from my father a little information about his early life. When I was grown and had been to the battlefield of Shiloh he did remark that his father and an uncle had fought there and that the uncle had been wounded. I somehow forgot to ask whether the wounded Confederate had been the brother of his father or of his mother. So I do not know now.

My father was not secretive, but somehow he had sealed off the past, his own past. In a strange way he was depersonalized. I cannot remember that he ever in his life said, "I feel bad," or "I feel good." Never in any fashion, did he remark on a purely personal feeling. Not even in an extremity of grief.

I must go back to my father's only remark about his mother. He and I were in an automobile driving west from the town of Hopkinsville, Kentucky, toward the village of Cerulean Springs, near the farm where each year I spent many summer months with my maternal grandfather. I must have then been about twelve years old and was at

recently learned from the same friend, she had not died in the babyhood of my father but after some ten years of marriage. My father, who had certainly been old enough to remember distinctly that mother, not only never referred to her, but presumably had as little pious interest in visiting her grave as he had for visiting that of his father. Certainly, this fact is in marked contrast to the respect, concern, and protection which he always showed for Grandma Jenny, the widow of a father whom he never, beyond two or three casual times, ever mentioned.

In sharp contrast, my father often referred to his brother Sam. He admired, looked up to, and loved Sam. The feeling seemed beyond any ordinary affection for a brother. As for Cortez, his other brother, I was always puzzled that he did not feel repulsion. My father, though he never introduced the name of Cortez into conversation, did pay an annual visit to him, a visit which, as far as I could know, was never discussed. Cortez was, in my view then, and now, a truly monstrous man, proudly ignorant, cheaply cynical, mean-spirited, cruel. On the one occasion when I, then grown up, gave my opinion of Cortez, my father merely replied: "That is probably because he cannot help it."

Whether Cortez could help it or not, he managed to reduce his wife to a cringing hag, and his only child, a beautiful and seemingly intelligent girl, into a totally stupid, totally uneducated, helpless creature, who had never been allowed, even when grown, to spend a night, or even a full day, away from him (I say "from him" for the cringing hag was long since dead).

I could never understand why my sister, who was extremely intelligent and soaked in books, would spend days with the daughter of Cortez and Cortez himself. After the death of Cortez, I allowed myself to tell her my opinion of the man. She merely said to me: "You should have seen him in his coffin. He looked so little." He had been a rather tall man, beginning long back to collapse into fat.

The end of the daughter might have been predictable. At the death of her father she turned her inheritance into cash and disappeared for years. She was finally found by relatives of her long-dead mother, I seem to remember, in the world of the riverfront of Paducah, Kentucky— the wreck of a drug addict. Now rescued, and returning from a hospital, she was simply a sort of gray blob of nothing in a white silk dressing gown. Thus I once saw her. Briefly. The hand offered me felt like a dead fish.

Sam must have been the opposite of the monster Cortez. About the time of some serious and mysterious event in my father's family, an event about which my father never uttered a word and I never uttered a question, Sam was old enough to disappear. All I ever heard is that he went first to Texas and then to Mexico, where he became a "mining man" and where he prospered enough to send to my mother (whom he had never seen) a handsome set of rubies ready for mounting to make a brooch, a ring, and the pendant for a necklace. There was my mother's exclamation of happy surprise, and the pleasure, not in words, of my father at Sam's act. I remember that fact.

I am pretty sure that the rubies were never used as directed. My mother already had several good diamond rings (one from her mother, I think) which she rarely wore except when she was sitting with my father. She must have sold the rubies along with the diamonds when the Depression first struck and he was feeling the pinch.

My most vivid memory concerning Sam is my coming, in daylight, into a shadowy room where my father, who should have been downtown at the little bank, was sitting in his big black leather chair, his head bowed on his chest, and the arm nearer me hanging limply over the chair, with a sheet of paper hanging from the obviously loose grip of fingers. I don't know how long I stood there before my father slowly lifted his head and stared at me before saying "Son, Sam is dead."

My father had obviously been weeping. I had never seen him weep. It was a real shock to me to know he would weep at all, at anything. I was to remember the reddened eyes.

Later I was told that Pancho Villa had raided the mine and that Sam, his wife, and son had escaped to New Mexico, where Sam died. I seem to remember that he had been wounded, but am far from certain. Many years later on a trip by automobile to California, I stopped at Albuquerque and tried to find the grave. There was a record of some sort at the office, but I can't remember anything beyond that point.

I do remember that Sam's widow (with a Spanish name, which now escapes me) was almost penniless then and that my father began to help her, and almost certainly put her son into a preparatory school, for there was in my family a photograph of the young man wearing some sort of school military uniform. The photograph was incribed by Sam's son to my father. In the late 1930s, long after my mother's death, my father on one of his wandering automobile trips, alone, drove west and saw his nephew for the first time. Sam's son was at a mine in Montana, where he was an engineer, and took my father on various tours. My father told me every detail.

As a kind of footnote to the story of Sam, I add that decades later I received a letter from the wife of the grandson of Sam with a clipping from a newspaper in Chicago or perhaps Minneapolis or Madison, a clipping, very long, the upper half or so of an inner page concerned with the national meeting of the Association of Mining Engineers—or something of the sort. Part of the clipping was a photograph of the recipient of a medal of the Association to a mining engineer for research and invention fundamentally important for the safety of mines. The recipient was Sam's grandson. My father was dead by that time.

Somehow I have usually assumed that my father considered his behavior in relation to Sam's family perfectly normal. As to what he would consider "normal" I usually have only my mother's accounts, my eavesdropping, or my logical deduction. But there is one instance which I clearly encountered.

Once, on one of the automobile trips with my father after my mother's death, we were driving in a section of Kentucky unfamiliar to me. He looked up from the map and directed me to take a certain road. We found, in the country though near a village, a newish brick building of some size, clearly not a dwelling. It proclaimed itself to be a clinic.

At the desk my father asked for a certain doctor. Very quickly a man, probably toward fifty years old, appeared. He literally seized my father's outthrust hand, uttering an exclamation of pleasure. It turned out that he was Doctor So-and-So—a name my father had never mentioned. He wanted to show my father the new clinic and called for a younger colleague to join us. He himself fell behind the colleague talking to my father, and joined me. He said he wanted to tell me something. His being there in that clinic, even having an education, he said in secret haste, was due to my father. My father, he said, had helped him years before when he had no hope. That must have been, I later decided, in the years when my father was trying to establish himself to marry my mother and when he was also playing father to the youngest of his step-siblings, my Uncle Ralph.

I cannot remember, perhaps never caught, the doctor's name.

I again have wandered from chronology. It must have been well into the 1880s when Sam took out for Mexico.

I had somehow always assumed that Sam took out because his father, W. H. Warren, had died. Even in a book-length narrative poem published in 1953 this is assumed by a character in the poem, "R.P.W.," who refers to the death of his father's father as at a certain time. This is not only bad calculation, but ignorance. Actually W. H. Warren died in 1893 and was buried in the cemetery of Cerulean Springs, Kentucky. The date of his death is given on the tombstone. Only lately a friend has told me this. I have never seen the stone.

Although my father, even if in bits and fragments, had told me something of Sam, he had never told me of his own father, W. H. Warren, the returned veteran. He is officially recorded as from Tennessee (actually from Kentucky, a divided state), and this fact distinguishes him from another W. H. Warren (a major) who earned fame by surrendering to an emissary of Sherman. For my grandfather Warren, a captain, there is no record of combat experience, but this fact, an experienced researcher has told me, could be regularly accounted for if he was in ordnance, such commands having been shifted as need required, with no record. Or he may, as another researcher has volunteered, have been on the staff of General Bragg, a poor place to be. But my father did once tell me that his father had fought at Shiloh—which was also an uncomfortable place to be.

Whatever his military record, one nonmilitary matter has been coming to my mind for years. During one of my boyhood visits to his widow, Grandma Jenny, I had been prowling, out of loneliness as much as curiosity, in an attic or "lumber room," as a place for discarded junk was called. There I found some strange-looking books. They seemed particularly strange in a house where there were no other books except the Bible and the local telephone directory. The strange new item was a translation, as it announced itself to be, from a writer whose name I had never heard of and did not know how to pronounce. It was spelled "D-a-n-t-e." This book had some strange pictures, and the name of the artist was again one which I did not know how to pronounce: "Doré." The other book was clearly *Paradise Lost*. I happened to know the name of the author, but the pictures, I seem to recall, were by the same man who had done the illustrations for the first and more mysterious book.

I puzzled over my discoveries, and finally took them to Grandma Jenny. She said: "Oh, those old books, they belonged to your grandfather. When he died, I just threw away such stuff with the other old stuff."

More than once I have wondered about the ownership of those old books. I have always been sure of what Grandma Jenny said. But did she really know that the books had belonged to her husband? I know of no additional evidence that he was a bookish man. Since her husband had died in 1893, my father, who would have already been embarked on his literary ambitions in Clarksville, may have brought such things with him when back to visit a dying father. Then, if he had forgotten his books on going back to Clarksville, his stepmother may well have thrown such items aside with the "stuff" left around by her dead husband. In any case the most recent edition of Carey's *Inferno* would have been available, even at secondhand. As would have been the *Paradise Lost* with the Doré illustrations. And the little town of Clarksville was a bookish place. I know that the work of Melville, before the publication and failure of *Moby Dick,* was widely read and discussed by the Gentleman's Literary Society of the town. In fact, at the Houghton Library, at Harvard, I have seen a letter to Melville from the secretary of the Clarksville Literary Society.

The event of my showing the books to Grandma Jenny may well have been the last time I was ever to visit her, years before the death of my mother on October 5,

1931. That day my father and I had stood in the hall outside of the operating room, not talking, simply waiting. Eventually the doctor came out. Not the surgeon. He was carrying something on a pad of gauze in the palm of his right hand. He offered it to my father's sight. My father looked studiously at the little blob of something on the gauze. It was streaked with blood. "There it is," the doctor said.

Without any words, my father and I walked back to the hospital waiting room ("parlor" it was called). There, my brother and sister were waiting. Wordlessly, we waited until the patient was returned from the recovery room. We were finally beckoned to go into her room.

After the stretcher had been wheeled in but before the patient had been placed in bed, she had been able to lift a hand in the briefest of greetings before it fell back. Then, transferred to the bed, she managed to smile. During the period thereafter—an indeterminate period—our father sat by the bed holding her right hand. Small and irrelevant facts may become vastly significant. I remember which hand. She was lying on her back.

Now and then she smiled at our father. He, except for those moments of the smile, sat erect as usual but with head bent a little toward her. I remember how the light shone on his bald head. When she smiled he managed what could then be his version of a smile. That version, however fleetingly, reminded me of the boyishly embarrassed smile he used to give when, at his birthday breakfast, she would pause in passing behind his chair and kiss him on top of the bald pate and call him her "comic valentine." At such moments he had always managed to say, "Oh, shucks."

He said nothing now.

He had never been, in fact, a man to express his feelings in words. I know that even as a child I had never felt any need of words from him beyond what an occasion of human pleasantness suggested. I am somehow sure that neither my sister nor brother ever felt differently. Off and on for years I have speculated what words he must have laid tongue to for Anna Ruth Penn when she was a girl, or a young wife.

Now in the hospital room I became aware that the doctor, with fingers on the patient's pulse, was nodding significantly to our father. The doctor wished to spare us the view of the last throes. If there were to be such.

Our father rose and leaned to give our mother the good-bye kiss. Then each of the children, in order of age, approached the bed. Her eyes were open, the face upward and smiling, momentarily bathed in a lost youthfulness.

I could not at that instant have seen the face when our father leaned, but I saw the face when I leaned, and then looked back as each—my sister, then my brother—came in turn.

When we four got back to the parlor, there was Grandma Jenny. Had she been there earlier? I cannot remember. In any case, there she was, sitting to one side, in a straight chair, erect but with head slightly bowed, seemingly unchanged by time, wearing the Sunday dress of black silk, with the faint glistening on it from electric light, turned on by now and not well shaded. Under the black skirt the black kid shoes, scarcely visible, were set side by side on the floor, as though in a showcase.

After my father, jerking himself erect, had walked to his seat (on an armless sofa, I think) Grandma Jenny came to him and laid a hand on his shoulder. No, I am not sure. Perhaps this event came only after the doctor, entering, had nodded his head to my father. Two things here blur for me. The most vivid recollection is that, when the doctor entered to give the fatal nod, my father stared at him and then, with unbending spine, suddenly collapsed sidewise. Was it then that the old lady came to reach down and lay a hand on the shoulder of the fallen man?

All that I have detailed violates general chronology. I suppose, however, that it may have a chronology of its own: a chronology of vividness and sequence, not of event, but of recollection. Now leaving that fallen body on the couch my mind turns to what literal chronology dictates: the early life of that fallen body there.

At the age when a boy begins to ask questions—say eleven or twelve—I once asked my father what he had done as a boy. I suddenly wanted to know anything, everything. I remember the very spot in our yard, beside a hedge, late one afternoon, and I remember the look on his face. It was a strange intense look. I must have had to ask him again. Then he said that once when he and Sam, his big brother, were around my age, they had gone into a field of youngish corn, say about four feet high, where each boy straddled a row and then moved forward to bend the stalks a little down, this for a "pretty long row." Did I then ask him what happened, or did he simply wait a long time before speaking? In any case, with not uncharacteristic brevity and understatement, he said: "Our father did not like it."

I can't now believe that I did not ask him what his father had done. Punished them? Given a whipping? What? But recollection goes no farther. I suppose that this fact has some significance, but exactly what I don't quite define.

We, the three children, knew for a certainty that children, not uncommonly, got whipped. But the very word had for us, at least for me, the fascination of mysterious obscenity. We knew mere punishment: no movie; if a party was in prospect, no party; nobody to play with; no visiting. But never anger, or even a real-to-goodness scolding, though there might well be a detached and rational description of the crime involved. But the real thing was some sense of a withdrawal, not actual, for nothing would actually change, no unusual word, always the usual smile, but something undefinably withdrawn.

Whatever I know about my father's childhood and youth is a few scattered fragments. At one time he told me that his father, at some time back from war, had had "a good deal" of land, but too much was "in forest" and had to be cleared by "slashing and burning"; and I had an imagined picture of young boys watching a forest fire. Certainly, at another period, my father, as he once told me, had "axed out" red oak cross ties for a railroad being laid in the region. But at what age? When? Where? Long ago in a poem I referred to a young axeman who kept repeating a simple Greek conjugation to himself. This is certainly wrong, for the Greek belonging to the story would certainly have come much later.

At some time along the way a local doctor, for whom my father had a job driving day or night, became his friend in a paternal way. In the end he even offered to pay for the young fellow's education if he would promise to come back and be a country physician. This benevolent friend even took the young fellow to visit a medical school (probably at Nashville, Tennessee). But after a time visiting dissection rooms the young fellow decided that his passion for learning did not go "that far." That was his phrase when he was fifty-odd years old.

The only episode of his youth which my father ever told me in detail must have occurred about this time. But the first detail of his narrative has never been clear to me. By one recollection I have it that my father was out fishing with another youth, and took refuge in a "large general store" against a sudden storm. The other recollection is that my father, very young, had some sort of job in the big country store. In any case a number of people suddenly took refuge in the store.

But the refuge was a death trap. The storm was a tornado. The big barn of a building crumpled. The roof and beams collapsed over the wreckage below. The weather having been unseasonably chill, a little fire was in the big stove (you can imagine the big potbellied iron stove, and how tobacco juice spattered there, long back or fresh, had crinkled dry and was now turning pale yellow on the hot iron). The fallen beams, boards, and roof shingles finally caught on fire.

The young fellow who was to be my father was there, but not, for the moment, trapped. There must have been a long set of counters, at least on one side, running the length of the building; and he must have been standing near those counters when the heavy rafters from the ridge of the roof to that side had fallen at right angles across the counters. The counters clearly had been sturdy enough to bear the weight and make a kind of little tunnel. The young fellow could crawl there even as he began to hear screams as the fire spread in the debris. And then a voice, a black man's voice, loud but self-controlled, was giving directions: "Git it off my laigs. Yeah, Boss, I'm all right. Jes laigs. Hurry up, Boss. Fahr's comen."

There was no boss there.

The young fellow crawling down his tunnel could push

his way through. Finally at a gap between counters he got between them and along the outer wall, until he found a gap crushed in the wall. But even once through the wall his escape was blocked, for a great part of the roof, still intact, had angled down to the ground outside.

Strength was going. But the young fellow saw a spot where only shingles were barring daylight. In a last effort he drove a fist through shingles and waved the hand back and forth.

As a boy I had heard of the bare facts of the tornado and an escape, but when my father was nearing eighty he received a letter. The letter was from a contemporary who, also a big boy then, had escaped from the burning ruin. This other old man now wrote his old acquaintance this letter, his account of the incident, and then a short summary of his own pleasant and modestly successful life. Looking back he felt the need to speak to the fellow survivor.

But there was an enclosure: the clipping, now yellowed with all the years, from a newspaper of Louisville, or perhaps Nashville, gave a rather detailed narrative of a "promising young man named Warren" whose hand, feebly waving from a hole in the collapsed roof, had been seen by a girl, the daughter of the local blacksmith whose shop was near the scene of the "tragedy." No romance was ever to round out the story.

My father showed me the yellowed clipping. He then again gave me, so many years after his first account, a fuller version, still cold and detached, but now including the anonymous voice of the Negro man whose legs had been pinned, even imitating the voice a little. I had never in my entire life heard him give any words bordering on the dramatic or imitative. His rare narratives had always seemed objective and factual.

Now he laid the clipping aside and, after I had looked at it, said nothing more on the subject. Later, after his death, I found it, then falling to pieces.

Later the "promising" young man left the country and had some sort of job in Clarksville, Tennessee, on the Cumberland River, then still a smallish town though it had been the first settlement in the state, founded in 1783. I do not know what kind of job the young man had there in 1890, but fairly soon he must have come on a pretty good one. Certainly, he had had little formal education, probably in that period and place, not more than a bad sixth grade. But certainly he had been reading what he could come by, and at one stage in Clarksville he must have made friends with a local lawyer and begun "reading law." As a boy I had seen in our house his copy of Blackstone and a few other such forbidding volumes. And he had obviously had access to books that were not trash.

In Clarksville, he began to assemble his own books. At this moment, now, I go to a shelf and take down Volume I of his set of Thackeray to check the flyleaf. "R.F. Warren, Clarksville, Tennessee, 1894." He had prospered enough to buy various such sets. I remember Bulwer-Lytton, Cooper, Thackeray, Dickens, even the forgotten "Ouida," and various volumes of poetry. After finishing a book he sometimes wrote at the end "Finished" with his initials and the date. Only a few sets, or even books, now survive to me.

As for poetry, he knew a great deal by heart, a fact I well remember from very early childhood. One of the first things I remember his reading to me was "Horatius at the Bridge." I made him read it over and over again, evening after evening. Finally his tireless indulgence snapped. He said: "Never mention that poem to me again. Take that book and go sit in a corner and look at every word and be reciting the poem to yourself while you look at the words. This will be reading." A few years later my favorite was "How They Brought the Good News from

Ghent to Aix." I have the vague notion that at some later time he read me "The Ancient Mariner"—though I may "remember" this merely because I had to read it more than once to my own very young son. He loved that and "Sir Patrick Spens" and often asked for them. Now, not too irrelevantly perhaps, I remember that he is mad for the sea, and has built his own schooner.

One of the few books of poetry that I find now, in the remnants of the long-past dispersal of my father's little library, is a collection of probably the worst poems ever put into print. The title is *The First Mortgage,* a series of seminarrative pieces dealing with high points of the Bible from Creation to the Ascension of Christ. My father's name is in place. The date is 1897. Perhaps the reason that I remember this book and have now sought it out is the name of the illustrator here: Gustave Doré. And perhaps the book had been bought because of the young man's acquaintance with the Doré of the old Dante and Milton.

The book could scarcely have been bought out of piety. To me as a big boy he once referred to himself as an "old-fashioned freethinker." As for the illustrations in the book, they are not quite so awful as the poems.

The young man of 1890, who turned twenty-one in

that year, must have had enormous energy and great hopes. One tiny piece of evidence goes back to my early childhood. Before breakfast I liked to watch him shaving, this with a big old-fashioned straight razor, a blade that, when not covered with lather, would flash like a saber as he expertly flung it about. There would be a satisfying sound as the blade whacked through the dark, stiff bristles. My father might talk to me a little or occasionally quote something, even as he shaved or while cleaning the razor. A few times over those years he simply seemed to be gabbling something. At one time, as he told me, what he was saying came from the opening of the Gospel of John. To the boy admiring the flash of the blade and the skill of the wielding hand the words coming forth were just a gabble. Then, cleaning the razor, the wielder remarked: "That's Greek. Now you know how it sounds."

He paused, and then made what must have been a private joke to himself, by himself, on himself: "I hope it is."

The episode puzzled me so much that it stuck vividly in my mind, the whole scene. Another time or two when he was ending his shave, he might gabble again. Those bits of gabble, he must have told me, were poetry.

Such tiny fragments may have been all the Greek that

still stuck in his head. Much later I gathered that he must have had some sort of tutor in Greek. How would he have tried to learn Greek alone? As a matter of fact there had been in Clarksville a very good little university, Southwestern Presbyterian University, with, of course, the teaching of Greek. The Presbyterians, unlike some Protestant sects, believed in an "educated clergy." Some sixty-odd years later, I found my father's Greek grammar and his lexicon (the famous old Liddell & Scott), that lexicon now being in the hands of his granddaughter, who has used it for many years. But most of his books had been lost many years earlier when, after my mother's death in 1931, he went bankrupt, losing his house and going to live in a rented room. There he had no place for books—and perhaps for a time no heart for them. Almost all books which he had owned had been flung away—perhaps by his own hand—to rot in the damp of some abandoned building on Main Street of the town. So my brother told me years later. But a few he had kept as required for his lonely evenings.

In Clarksville, French had been a sort of footnote to the Greek. During my college years about 1923, when my father and I were on some errand to Clarksville, a bigger place by then, he asked me to come with him to greet a friend from the "old time." We entered a prosperous-looking men's clothing store, where my father asked for Mr. So-and-So. The clerk disappeared, and another man, gray-haired and older than my father, came hurrying toward us. After the greeting the man turned to me, shaking hands, then patting me on the shoulder. My father said: "Son, I wanted you to meet my old French teacher." Then the man lured me into my garbled French.

I was never to see my father's old friend again. I seem to remember that he was an Alsatian who, after his schooling, had come to America to seek his fortune. Perhaps the nice store may have been his fortune. I was never to hear his name again. Such silence was, of course, characteristic of the man's old pupil. But the several histories of France around my boyhood house may well have been testimony to that sealed-off time.

Even earlier than that hint of the past, probably when I was about eleven or twelve, I was idly prowling in a bookcase and happened to find, flat against the wall behind other books in proper places, a thick black volume. The title was *The Poets of America*. I certainly had no particular interest in poetry, but I idly happened to open the book. By accident—or was there a reason why the book came open there?—it had opened to a page with the name of my father in print across the top. Below, at the head of the left column on that page there was a photograph of my father as a young man. He must then have been about twenty-two or perhaps twenty-three. There were several poems on the page. His poems. The discovery was, in itself, a profound and complex surprise. Of what nature I cannot remember.

I could not wait for my father to come home. When he did get there I showed him the book. He took it, examined it, and wordlessly walked away with it. That was the last time I was ever to see it.

Many years later, long after his death, I happened to mention the episode to a friend. Later the friend sent me a photostat of the title page of the book and of the page of the photograph and the poems. He had advertised for the book and bought a copy of what must have been that old "vanity publication." I was later to learn that my sister, a little younger than I, had finally encountered the book again hidden by our father, and had simply, as she said, "stolen" it. He had not managed to destroy it, after all.

Long after my father had walked away with the book, some thirty years after, when he was in his seventies, I received a letter from him. No, not a letter, a sheet of paper in a modern pre-stamped business envelope. But the sheet was of typing paper yellowing, even flaking, with age. The poem typed there was in the purple ink of a typewriter ribbon of that early period. Beneath the poem was typed the signature "R.F.W." The signature was also from the archaic purple ribbon. But at the lower edge of the sheet were, in a scribble of old age, the words: "Do not answer."

As a boy I found two other relics of the period in Clarksville. First, there was a military cartridge belt with the scabbard of a bayonet attached, I think, to the belt. In spite of all efforts, I think, I could never find the bayonet. I tried to wear the belt as it was, but it was, of course, too big. So I swung it over my left shoulder to hang with the scabbard on my right side.

Under questioning, my father said that he had joined the National Guard. I asked him why. He seemed to be thinking the matter over. Then he said that it had merely been something new, that he had liked the drill and the friends. Then he suddenly added that when the Spanish-American War came the Tennessee Guard was called up. His term of enlistment was long over, but he went down to wave goodbye to his company.

The main event of that period of the life of Robert

Franklin Warren was his acquaintance with a young girl, Anna Ruth Penn, who was to become his wife. A fact that has seemed more and more odd to me in idle recollection is the growing awareness that the family of W.H. Warren and that of my maternal grandfather Gabriel Thomas Penn seem to have had at best only a speaking acquaintance. The fact once seemed odd to me because both were veteran cavalry officers of Tennessee commands, even though W.H. Warren was a Kentuckian. But it was a big army.

For a time I assumed that W.H. Warren had died long before Grandpa Penn had settled in south Kentucky, but in recent years I have learned that W.H. Warren had died in 1893 and that his tombstone still stands in the cemetery of Cerulean Springs within little more than a rifle shot of the farm of Grandpa Penn, where summer after summer my father would come to visit before taking his family back home to Guthrie. Why had my father never even mentioned the fact to me? Or why never taken me on at least one pious pilgrimage to see the stone of my other grandfather—his own father?

Later on, to add to oddness, I learned that my father had first come to the house of Anna Ruth as a friend of her older brother, who was the age of the suitor-to-be.

By this time my father must have been living in Clarksville, and perhaps had come back to Cerulean Springs only for the illness or death of his father.

The Penns had only become Kentuckians by accident. With his company, back in the early days of the Civil War, Captain Penn had hanged some "bushwhackers," as guerrillas—outlaws using some military excuse for outlawry—were commonly called. After the war when Grandpa Penn came home to Tennessee and got married and had a son, the heirs of local bushwhackers, now all good unionists as circumstances naturally dictated, went to law as well as to violence for revenge. So Grandfather Penn fled to Kentucky and settled. Either going with him or arriving later was his old nurse, Aunt Cat, whom I have been tempted to say that I had seen as a child. I am not at all sure that I did not, for the image in all sorts of detail is vivid to me. But the image may come from the frequent references to her by my grandfather, my grandaunt Anna, or my aunts and mother. In any case she must have been very old, for my grandfather had been born in 1836.

For a time Gabriel Thomas Penn apparently prospered, not only as a tobacco grower but as a "buyer"—an agent who would take tobacco on consignment from growers and market it after it had been graded. But Grandpa Penn was, as his daughters never forgot to say, "visionary," and missed a payment on an insurance installment on a storage barn. That is a tale I remember. He paid the loss, but his family, and everybody else it seems, decided that he had no head for business.

This visionary Penn, as I have said, was not even a Kentuckian, and though born and raised in Tennessee was of Virginia stock running back to the early days. What I do remember about my mother's family I remember in patches from a bulky record left by my Aunt Mary Mexico Penn. ("Mexico" being, of course, in honor of some kinsman who, in the Mexican War, had distinguished himself at least enough for family purposes.) Aunt Mary was, of course, a spinster: I have noticed that family records are always in the hands of a spinster, who doesn't have enough trouble with the present to disburb attention to the past.

I certainly never read all of Aunt Mary's book, and about all I remember are the Revolutionary War and a bit of the Civil War in Virginia. There was Colonel Abram Penn, who for his military service had a sound land grant near, or including, the present city of Roanoke. His name found a dubious immortality as the name of the north-south highway passing through that city. At least the highway bore that name when I last drove over it some thirty-odd years back. A certain John Penn, uncle or cousin of the warrior, bears the less dubious distinction of being the only "Signer" (for North Carolina) of whom no portrait remains. At least that distinction had not been challenged in 1944 when, in a fever of patriotism, the Library of Congress tried to collect portraits of such worthies.

The burden of genealogy lay lightly over the summer gatherings at the farm at Cerulean Springs, but it was there that I sensed the meaning of family, the old man, my father, my mother, Aunt Mary, a younger aunt with a husband and children, and visits to the place of my great-aunt Anna, my grandfather's sister-in-law, where hung his portrait as a young man before the Civil War, a life size bust, in color, very true to life—probably painted by some wandering artist back in the Tennessee days, the kind of artist who moved from farm to farm peddling his wares. How vividly I remember the shock I had when I first began to compare that handsome and youthful portrait with the old man before me.

Grandpa's house gave me my impression of a "home place"—the vital center of life. But I soon began to realize that it was a home place only for me, and in a very special way. Nobody ever came there except on business, and business was always cut brief. Only one family ever came to dinner: a widow named Rawls with a son I played with, and a grown (or growing) daughter who studied elocution. I finally understood why that family came to dinner on Sunday. The gifted daughter was supposed to recite my grandfather's favorite poems by the hour, with appropriate gestures and stances. And this too often meant that her brother and I had to squirm for hours before we could break for the woods.

But the Rawls's visit was the only social event of the summer. My father, who, at the end of summer, customarily came for a visit to the Penn place, would wind up summer by taking a day off to go and see his kin, his stepmother and the monstrous Cortez.

In a way I almost resented my own father's visit to the Penns. In the months before he came I had the grandfather to myself. He might sit for hours under his favorite cedar tree, thinking his thoughts, but often he talked with me. The sisters might be at some distance, sewing or gossiping under a stand of maples, out of earshot. Occasionally the old man would seize the opportunity of quoting poetry to me, things he happened to dredge up from years before. One piece by a forgotten early American poet began:

> At midnight, in his guarded tent,
>   The Turk was dreaming of the hour
> When Greece, her knees in suppliance bent,
>   Should tremble at his power.

The poem goes on to the bloody midnight when the great Greek hero Marco Bozzaris, bursts upon the camp:

> Come to the bridal-chamber, Death!

But much of Byron was quoted, most memorably "The Isles of Greece," or from *Childe Harold,* in which thunder in the Alps would burst

> . . . from peak to peak
> The rattling crags among . . .

There were tiny bits of Pope and an incalculable amount of Burns. In fact, the old man had seemed to take up where my father had left off.

As for his old war, there were anecdotes, often strange or humorous, not bloody. When I was big enough to understand, more or less, he talked about his views when the Civil War was coming on. He had then been against the States Rights notion because, he said, his "people" had fought in the Revolution to make a country and he did not want to see that country "Balkanized." And he thought that slavery was an "outmoded" (or was it "outgrown"?) institution (or "practice" or something). But when the War came and Virginia was invaded, he was ready to fight. Now, in our age, how strange it seems that people who had never even seen Virginia often felt themselves to be, somehow, Virginians. But this was still true in the 1920s of some few families whose connections with Virginia were by then much more tenuous than those of my grandfather.

Now and then he might resume talk of other bits of history, usually from Napoleon's campaigns, illustrated by a map which the point of his stick would scratch in the ground. Often, for documentation, there were references to an old book, *Napoleon and his Marshals*. But in my last summer with him he wanted me to read to him from *A History of Egypt* by Breasted (published in 1916).

In any case he seemed, in his way, to share many of my father's tastes. Certainly, it seemed so when, in my father's summer visits, the two might sit together, engrossed in their private conversation, totally intent on whatever the subject might be. At various times I might appear to be wandering aimlessly past, but I was always trying to hear that mysterious conversation. But whenever I came close I had the distinct impression that the old conversation had been dropped in favor of some remark on the weather or crops. Or in favor of silence.

Many years later, in looking back on those two men, I began to have the feeling that their peculiar companionship was that of men who had lived beyond striving and hope into the peace of looking back with a gentle detachment—but with pity, love, or irony when such might be due. In short, the notion began to grow that their peculiar bond was based on failure: one who had failed because he was a "visionary," the other who had laid aside ambition in favor of another aspiration. Each in his own way seemed to be watching an old inflamed strenuosity sink calmly into the general human condition.

There was another remark among the daughters which seemed related to the notion that the old man was a visionary. They had said, more than once in their protracted and loving diagnosis of their father, that he was a "*Confederate* reader." Or so it seemed. I would wonder what a "Confederate reader" might be. But as my vocabulary widened, it suddenly dawned on me that the old man was an "inveterate reader." In fact, he was. As long as eyes held out.

But two of the three sisters were also such. In fact, my mother, Ruth, was one. The first Shakespeare I ever read was from her well-thumbed, multivolumed, green-backed set of Shakespeare (which I still have). The first thing I ever read of Shakespeare was from this set, and a very disappointing work it was—*The Rape of Lucrece*.

The owner of those numerous green-backed little volumes must have been an extremely pretty and graceful girl. My chief piece of evidence is a photograph which I found among my father's papers after his death. At the time of the picture she must have been toward twenty years old.

Long after my mother's death, my father, in an odd moment of recollection, remarked that he had married before he was "properly established." But it would not have been "fair" to make her wait longer. Or to make himself wait longer. They were married in 1904.

Since my father had not felt himself "established," he had put aside earlier ambitions at Clarksville to move to a new town which had great promise, a few miles away up in Kentucky. There everything seemed promising. I now hold in my hand a full and long-yellowing sheet of the *Evening Post* of Louisville, Kentucky, of April 18, 1903. A glamorous future is promised at the new crossing of North-South and East-West railway lines, with twenty-two train stops a day, two new banks, and "three saloons." In addition there was a mile-long race track with stables, bleachers, water, view, and breeding farms. "Many fine horses are bred here," the *Evening Post* affirms.

So there came Guthrie, on the edge of a region called Pondy Woods, with good farm country to back it on three sides. It was a brilliant idea, too, to name the town Guthrie, for a Mr. Guthrie who is said to have been the president, or something important, of the railroad. But the idea did not pay off. The ungrateful Mr. Guthrie never gave the town a railroad "roundhouse," and only a generation later did the town get a "creosote plant" for treating cross ties.

I do not know what my father first did at Guthrie, but his picture is on that yellowing sheet of the *Evening Post* as one of the founders and cashier of the new bank. He may have had a store there, too, and I remember that during the years of my childhood and youth while he operated the bank, he owned a store, and, I think, did some trading in farmland. In any case, at home he never talked about anything that "went on out there."

For a time before his marriage he lived in Guthrie, with a younger half brother to whom he actually played the role of father. The town was, in fact, having a period of prosperity. A large hotel was built at the new railroad station, with a newsstand where later you could come by the *New Republic* or *Poetry* magazine, if you were that ilk of traveler. A more convincing piece of evidence of prosperity is a photograph I yet own, the view from some high spot (the water tower of a railroad probably) on the day when the town was crowded with 25,000 visitors on horseback, in carriages, in farm wagons, on foot—there for the founding of the Black Fired Tobacco Association to combat price-fixing agreements among tobacco manufacturers. This precipitated the "Tobacco War," or "The Black Patch War," and another newsworthy gathering in Guthrie. My father took me, scarcely an infant, to see the troops putting up their tents in an open section near the railroad station.

The hotel has long since been demolished. Some of the stores on Main Street are abandoned. A big highway two miles off had skipped the town, and businesses that catered to that heavy traffic had moved toward customers.

Some of the more pretentious residences, well and solidly built, are sometimes empty. The automobile and the good road have been hard on many of the old "market towns." The stands and stables of the old race track had rotted down even in my childhood, before good roads and the automobile had done their work, and the track had gone to weeds. For generations there had been no more "sporting farmers" who bred and raced a few horses. Naturally the "Pennyroyal" section could not compete with the Blue Grass, but for a time, so the talk went in my childhood, the local world would send horses, "swabs," jockeys, and a manager up to fairs in the Middle West. The manager was said to have carried a general purse to make bets for stay-at-homes.

Even when I was a child the local track had been abandoned. There, on summer afternoons, my father was taking lessons in driving his first car—a "touring car" with acetylene headlights that to me seemed as big as washtubs, with brass rods everywhere, and a leather top that creaked and banged and "whooshed" as soon as the speedometer struck twenty. On a few afternoons my father would drive the monster around and around the old race track for an hour or two under the tutelage of the local blacksmith, who doubled as the only mechanic in that end of the county. My mother and I, she swathed in scarves and a veil, would be in the back seat with the younger children.

As for the marriage of our parents, none could have been more like what in earlier times had been called a "love-match." I never heard a cross word between them or even a telltale rise of tone in any of what they called "discussions"—to use the word they used. Once or twice, as a child, I overheard my mother say to some friend, or to a sister, something like this: "Oh, yes, a happy marriage is simple. Everything outside the front gate is Bob's concern and everything inside is mine." Then she would laugh.

Whatever magic formula our mother and father had discovered, they seemed to be engaged in a continuing private conversation. At night, after the children were in bed, I, the last to go, might hear the voices from the farther room, where, in winter, our parents would sit by the dying coals. It was only a murmur of voices, with occasional silences. I had to wonder what they were talking about.

On our picnics to the woods, this in times before the automobile when our father would have to rent a surrey from the livery stable, the same old conversation seemed to be picked up again. After the picnic fire had caught, and the picnic had been eaten, the pair might wander off, leaving the children to play or, if the season was right, to hunt nuts. Casually, the two would walk away, side by side, perhaps holding hands, their heads slightly bowed in conversation as they disappeared into the woods.

The word *surrey* reminds me how our father, in the days before the automobile, might rent one for a weekend to go visiting to the place of some friends in the country. There we would find all the animals, and you might be set high on a saddle alone up there while some son or farmhand led the quite safe and listless old creature. Or the host might swing to the saddle of a more spirited mount and hold you in front of him as you galloped around the pasture. You might even go fishing.

Only years later did I realize how cut off our family had been. I had been told that long back there had been a Ladies Literary Society in Guthrie, but later I have always found the idea hard to accept. Certainly the society did not survive into my time of memory, and in general my mother was a nonjoiner. In my earliest childhood my mother's closest friends were two ladies, a bit older than she, both from the country. My mother and the guest would dawdle over a cup of tea for some three hours. One of the guests would come in a buggy, which often she drove herself, the other in a big red Lincoln which moved limping and lumping over unpaved road. By and large the life of the family was at home or on long summer visits to the house of my grandfather.

At home, life was so perfectly organized that then I did not realize that it was organized at all. In the evenings of the early years one parent read to a child, or children, while the other was occupied by a book or magazine. Later, when I was in school, our mother read to the smaller children while our father read to me. The first prose book I remember was *A Child's History of Greece,* a grayish book with small fleurs-de-lis on the cover and fine pictures inside. For school work there was a study period absolutely observed, five nights a week, except for an occasional Friday night—which had to be made up on the weekend. For the study period there was always a parent present to answer questions and hear recitations. Sometimes, in the course of human events, there might be sleepiness or momentary rebellion, but the process never seemed a protracted tyranny. At school some classmate might tease, now and then in a nasty way, or some bolder characters might affirm that nobody was ever going to boss them "that-a-way." But for us the whole matter was rather like the weather, or life itself. It was the way things were. Or in a longer view, it must have been the tone of things that made all the difference.

One matter in this regard stands out in my memory: the serious and never condescending way a question from one of us would be treated. For instance, after the reading from the history of Greece and then that of Rome in the same series, I asked by father "whose side" should you be on in a history book. He seriously considered the question, said that it was a real question, and after a moment added that, as far as he could see, you might try to be on the side of the people you were at the time reading about. That satisfied me then, and I suppose that, in a sense, it still does.

Life, however, did not begin or stop at a schoolroom. Children came to play. Later there was a crude baseball diamond laid out by our father on some land near the house. I had a catcher's mitt, but I gave up that position after a week or so. The pitcher, my friend then and all his life, was later to pitch for the New York Giants, and even then I chose to stand about fifty feet behind home plate for the few afternoons before I was demoted to left field.

All those years, so unobtrusively that it could scarcely be noticed, my father followed the shifting interests of each child. My pitcher friend was already a real woodsman, and so I took to the woods with him. A little later appeared in our house a book by Ernest Thompson Seton, *Two Little Savages and How They Grew*. Later, when interest began to focus on birds, there appeared one Christmas a very good pair of binoculars. So on to animals. And when I tried to do sketches or watercolors of birds and animals, and got disgusted with my efforts, there happened to be the arrangement for me to spend some months of a summer with a family my mother knew in Nashville. There I was to take lessons from a nun at the Convent of Saint Cecilia, from Sister Mary Luke, who at the Chicago World's Fair had won the Gold Medal for watercolor. Soon she would be taking me by streetcar to the Glendale Zoo.

Sister Mary Luke and I would have a great hamper of delicacies on which the kitchen nuns had lavished their best talents. At the zoo Sister Mary Luke, a very small woman, would find a good tree for shade, lie on her back, go to sleep, and snore like a horse. I have never forgotten her toes sticking from under her ample, yellowish, sand-colored Franciscan skirts, toes in little black kid shoes pointing at the sky.

But things other than watercolor and birds came along,

including chemistry sets, manuals of electricity, the Morse code, and a homemade radio set which, even in a brief self-deception of glory, did not work. There was even a book on geology and a collection, soon forgotten. My father was a model of patience for us all, but he and I finally reached a collision point.

For some years after I was old enough my father had taken me for a Thanksgiving Day in Nashville. There he and I would have our fine private Thanksgiving dinner. Then always came the Thanksgiving Day football game of Vanderbilt University. After the game we might wander a little about the campus. He might casually point out the Law School. But in the end came the collision.

I wanted the Navy, for reasons too complex to go into here. My preference was confirmed after the father of an old friend of my mother, a certain "Professor" Dietrich, wrote to ask if she would meet his son when the train stopped at Guthrie for water. The son, he added, had just graduated from Annapolis, and would be warned that my mother would be at the station to meet him. The train arrived, and from the Pullman there descended a tall young man in summer whites, with epaulets and brass buttons. He kissed my mother on both cheeks, shook hands with my father, and gave me a manly handshake. My doom was sealed.

To that brief meeting there must be a footnote. Toward the end of the Korean War, I briefly visited, in London, a much younger friend who had distinguished himself in World War II at Anzio, and who was now stationed luxuriously as a naval attaché. He gave me a little Navy party. One guest was an admiral of some fifty-odd years. His name—Dietrich—struck me as peculiarly familiar. Later I rejoined him to ask if he had been born in Hopkinsville, Kentucky. He said: "How did you know?"

Long before that party my father had surrendered on the question of my studying law. He had made arrangements with our congressman, R.Y. Thomas, to exercise his privilege to make an appointment to Annapolis. Before "R.Y." could act he wanted me to have a physical examination. This was satisfactory. Somewhat later I had an accident which prevented my naval career. I was not a captain at the Battle of Midway.

At the university it was not to be the preliminary to studies for law but a chemistry major. After one term it was literature, without question. My father said nothing, and I did not then remember how his own life had run.

But that fact came sharply to me two or three years later when John Crowe Ransom, whose courses I had been taking at Vanderbilt University and whose poetry was then in full stride, was on a weekend visit to my house in Guthrie, along with one or two other friends. My father was sitting with us on a blanket under a maple tree. There, each of us would read a poem of personal preference from Thomas Hardy. When Ransom's turn came, he read "Wessex Heights."

I saw my father's deep response to that. Earlier John and my father had hit it off splendidly, going aside for conversations. The fact that John's education had always been primarily in Greek would have given him a special luster in my father's eyes, but, too, there were John's poems. I suppose that on this occasion, in the presence of John and my father, it really occurred to me why my father had so easily surrendered to me for not accepting the study of law.

My father had known what it was to sweat over poems. I had long since seen the hidden book. A couple of years before the scene on the blanket under the maple, I had begun to publish what I hoped were poems, the first in the fall or winter of 1922. A few others came along; one of them, in some sort of reflex against the triple names of many nineteenth-century authors, was signed "Penn Warren." My father had read the poem and made a friendly but critical remark. Then, still holding the little magazine (what, I forget), he asked me whether I did not like the name "Robert." With an instant of shame—it must have been shame—I remembered that he had once signed his full name.

One form of my father's attentiveness to my sister and me concerned the Bible. But, as I have earlier remarked, I had once heard him say that he "reckoned" he was an "old-fashioned freethinker." And he once said that the church (any Christian church, he must have meant) was a "useful social institution." In any case, he offered a gold piece—five or ten dollars, I don't remember—if I would read the Bible through. That could be done at three chapters a day with four on the first day of the next year. (Or is my remembered arithmetic at fault?) As though by way of afterthought, he added that the Bible was necessary to understand "our civilization." I got my gold piece. I still do not understand our civilization, but the project had been interesting, and in the next several years I read it again, now leaving out the dull parts of the Old Testament.

My father did finally join a church, the Methodist,

probably under some sort of social pressure. At home there was never any formal observance of any kind. For years children said the Lord's Prayer at the mother's knee and called for blessings, by name, on certain "kinfolks" or friends. After these years, prayer was never mentioned. There was never a grace at any meal. My father sent the children to Sunday school because, as he had once said, you could learn certain things there. But church was not compulsory. Apparently, he trusted Sunday school cards more than he did the minister. But he and my mother usually went to church on Sunday morning. Long after the death of my mother I definitely found out that she had been severely criticized in town for not "doing any church work."

If my father never showed any particular interest in church even as a "social institution," he showed a devoted interest in another social institution: education. For years he was very active on the school board. He wanted to know every detail about the training and personality of any applicant, and particularly of a possible principal or associate principal. At home there was never even a hint of such matters, but the fact was clear. The school which I attended through the twelfth grade had some remarkably good teachers. Education, my father said, but not in great originality, was the only salvation for democracy.

In spite of those good teachers of the school, the job of male principal was not easy. It involved more than a mere degree from the University of Kentucky. The principal had to be able to handle a rebel, almost always the biggest fellow in school. I once saw this happen. The principal, young, thin, tall, and somewhat tubercular-looking, was challenged by a big fellow who, for this account, shall remain nameless. The principal was at the blackboard explaining something. The big fellow, with appropriate noise, left his seat, drew up a chair to the unlighted iron stove, and propped up his feet on its support. The principal politely asked him to go back to his seat "quietly." In the end, the tubercular-looking principal belied his looks by speed, dexterity, and hidden brawn, and with a firm clutch on the belt or the seat of the fellow's pants, heaved the substantial burden through a window some half a story above the ground. Next day the loser, fresh as a daisy, was back in his seat, and at recess said that he had hit running and had run all the way to town looking back now and then "to be sure the bastard wasn't following me."

Suddenly in 1917 all violence at school stopped. Even the most burly champion of student rights couldn't quite bring himself to pick a fist fight with a nice old lady who, with World War I, had become principal. Chivalry may have been ailing but it was not dead. And even in the roughest time there had been some very good teachers. Even poems had to be memorized and recited and in high school Caesar had to be parsed.

After the early years, when there had been visits to friends in the country, our parents rarely went out. This is not to say that they were not generally friendly and sociable. My father knew everybody in what he called his "sidewalk friendships." And for years he would stop on his afternoon walk home to play checkers with old Mr. Morgan, who in good weather always sat on his porch waiting for "Bob" to come, the checkerboard already set up. Two games were my father's ration. Of these Bob always planned to lose half. There was another old man with whom he often stopped for a couple of games.

Somehow our mother knew everybody in that end of the county, and somehow, on the street, in stores, God knows where, she had acquired an encyclopedic knowledge of all lives around, every private and tiny detail of life. People found themselves telling her things as she stood, faintly nodding, faintly smiling. For one thing, "Miss Ruth" never gossiped. A confidence, something that had burst out to her, was just a stone down a well.

My father and mother must have known every baby or little child in town. I remember a particularly splendid little boy whom my father admired. My father loved to tell a tale about that "curly-headed character." Once when the little boy was barely old enough to push himself in a coaster wagon back and forth on a little patch of concrete walk, my father had stopped to pat him on the head. The child, sitting ferociously up, said, "Go way, you ole son-a-bitch. Don't go touchen me."

Now it seems that after a certain period my parents gravitated to the very young or the very old. Certainly, my father did. I do not try to explain this fact. Both my father and mother had had close friends of their own age, as was clear from many references and tales. There was one friend of the old time when my father had been reading Blackstone and such, a friend who had had no interest except law and who was to have a very successful career. For years and years he and my father never saw each other but kept up a correspondence, about what my father never said. Merely "he and I were friends a long time back." After I was long since grown and my mother dead, and I was back on a visit to my father, he asked me if I would drive him somewhere for an afternoon.

On our way, he said that So-and-So would not last much longer. We spent a couple of hours with that friend, now feeble and in a wheelchair. The room was shadowy, curtains almost drawn, but a floor lamp behind the wheelchair shed some light. One of the two old men might mention a name, a place, or even an obscure event, or a book. The other would remember—or could not. If remembrance came, there would be a fragment of conversation, always meaningless to me off in my shadowy corner. At last the head of the man in the wheelchair drooped down, chin on chest, eyes closed for some seconds or a minute. At last my father rose, went to him, and put forth his hand. The man took it and looked up at the face as though he could not recognize it, or was not sure. There must have been more, but I don't remember. That is a tableau in my head.

Such echoes of the past were very rare. For my mother as well as my father, a characteristic image, I must repeat, is that of the two walking somewhere—perhaps an image from those early picnics when they would wander off into the woods. The heads would be slightly bowed as though they were trapped in an interminable conversation never finished, and always there waiting to be resumed.

What were they talking about? I have no idea. Our mother was very affectionate to the children and to our father. He was not a demonstrative man, not even to his children. He did not have to be. His whole life was a kind of demonstration clearly understood. But I vividly remember his face when, thinking himself unobserved, he once leaned over the bed where my little brother lay ill. He was not seriously ill.

Self-control is a single quality that for my father seemed to underlie everything. Self-control was to survive even the death of his wife and, a little later, his bankruptcy. That quality was the mark of his life especially in the years when he lived in a rather drab rented room in walking distance of the house of my much younger brother, Thomas, and in decent weather in walking distance of the grave of his wife.

When little more than a boy, Thomas, who had dropped out of college after the death of our mother, had created a very thriving business, and badly needed somebody to manage the "inside" while he exploited his talent for the "outside." He persuaded his father to take over.

In all ways it was a perfect arrangement, but our father insisted on a minimum salary. His pride had already blocked a project that my brother and I had had of building a little house with quarters—inside or out—for some couple to take care of housekeeping and meals and chores.

But our father, in that crazy pride, had stayed in his room, walked into town for his picked-up and lonely meals, and, except when Thomas might come by, read at night. For he had begun again to accumulate some books. Thus he waited for the ritual dinner on Sunday, when he could see his three little granddaughters. I remember one Sunday when I was on a visit. Amid the scattered sheets of the big Sunday newspaper, he was sitting on a couch with a little girl some eight or nine years old, to whom he was teaching the first conjugation in Latin. She would keep repeating *"amo, amas, amat, amamus. . . ."* Then she would burst into gales of laughter.

It was so crazy she said. Then she would scream for more. Years later that little girl, at the university, was mad for French literature, and was to live in France for many years until her untimely death.

About the time of that visit, well after I had truly

discovered my father, he was visiting me in Louisiana. Before coming to my house, he wanted to explore New Orleans for himself. When he arrived I met him briefly there. I asked him why he hadn't put up in a hotel nearer to Frenchtown. He said that the place where he had put up was very good and comfortable, and added that it was more reasonable because of the distance. Anyway, he like to walk.

He examined me in what for the moment seemed a cool and detached way, and then said: "The first thing a man should do is to learn to deny himself."

There was a shock to that remark, perhaps because I was suddenly aware of all past self-indulgence.

He had not, of course, spoken to me. How the silence was broken, I cannot remember, but the conviction solidly grew that he was speaking of his whole life.

Some days later my father came to visit me in Baton Rouge. There an old friend of mine gave us a little dinner, some eight or nine people at the table. This was the day after news of Pearl Harbor had interrupted the Sunday dinner at my house. Now all conversation was the new war.

At last the hostess turned to my father and asked his opinion.

He thanked her, somewhat humorously, then said: "When one reaches my age he realizes how little his opinions mean. The world goes driving on its own way."

I left Baton Rouge for good in June, 1942. My father was never to come to my house again. It was not merely distance or war, and I often visited him. He was to survive the war a long time, and after the war he and I took various trips together, short and long.

The first was to Smithland, a village where the Tennessee River joins the Ohio. Toward two hundred years ago it had been a little river port with a promising future, but in the late 1940s was a forgotten spot. Near here the sister of Thomas Jefferson and her husband had once settled, and their two sons had been involved in the hideous butchery of a slave boy. I thought this was a natural symbol, and wanted to know the very spot where lay the ruins of their house.

My father and I drove there, northwestward from our town, skirting the land of his childhood. While driving to Smithland, he was extraordinarily attentive to the country, but said nothing of relevance. Near Smithland I found the track, not even a path, up the bluff to the site of the terrible house. My father drowsed in the car until I came back.

Later as we drove homeward, again through the land of his childhood, he was stirred to say that his father had, in the spring, always lined up the boys. "We were a house of boys," he said. This was to get a dose of an old remedy, crushed "percoon" steeped for months in whiskey, supposedly a medicine to "unthicken the blood of boys," and "keep them from meanness." My father could not remember what plant "percoon" was. For years I had never remembered at a convenient time to ask a botanist. But lately several have written to me.

This triviality seemed very important to me, something about a past that was a mystery. The trivial matter finally had to enter a book, a long narrative-dramatic poem, *Brother to Dragons.*

Another trip with my father, the last one, was to Mexico. Even in childhood, though without reflection, I had sensed his appetite to see the world. I had sensed it long back from the way he would talk of places which he had visited, or from the stories read to me, or to the other children. It could be sensed, too, from the way he spoke of certain novels he had read in the period of Clarksville, or from accounts of trips then taken.

For instance, he had been in New York and in Chicago at the time of the World's Fair. He must have been in

St. Louis at the time of the Louisiana Purchase Exposition, for he had seen, unless my memory is totally at fault, the famous Indian warrior, Geronimo, who had caused the United States army great trouble, and whose name reenters history in the cry of American paratroopers as they peel off. (Or so it is sometimes reported.) Geronimo, according to a ghosted autobiography, was indeed at the Exposition, where he sold photographs and autographs to crowds, and averaged a take of some two dollars a day. But the Exposition was in 1904, the year of the marriage of our parents. Could St. Louis have been on a wedding trip? There is no way of knowing. But one thing I do know. After I, the eldest child, had become a big boy, our father never even mentioned, in any way, his trips.

When he and I took our last trip together, in 1952, to Mexico City, he became as vigorous as a boy, and as full of all kinds of curiosity. His big brother, Sam, had been there, and that fact seemed to have made all the difference.

At Mexico City we put up at a pleasant hotel where I had once stayed for a time. His energy was appalling. We saw bull fights, frescoes, jai alai games, bars, restaurants, markets, museums, the mountains. He loved jai alai and wanted to see a game every night. I had assumed that he would want to visit mines where Sam had once been, and Guadalajara, where Sam had once lived and where I had often been during a long stay at Chapala. It would have been easy to go. Get a car in Mexico City and take the spectacular route west. But somehow my father kept postponing the idea. Until it was too late. I never guessed why. So we flew to Cuba.

Now, however, the most persistent recollection I have of our last trip is a moment when I woke up in our hotel room in Mexico City, about two or three in the morning. Somehow a very faint light, not more than a dimness, penetrated through the blinds. Only with effort could I make out the figure in the other bed, some six or seven feet away. The figure never moved. I was still lying awake when I heard a very faint sound, so faint that it could scarcely be called sound. But it was. And was, I suddenly realized, words.

Then I realized that the words were the tail end of a poem. It was a poem which I now cannot identify. Then after a long silence, came another poem in that same hushed susurrus. I recognized this one, a poem I had not seen or thought of since boyhood, but a great favorite which I had often made him read to me. It was about the burial of Sir John Moore, a hero killed during the

Peninsular War against Napoleon, when the English troops were about to evacuate their coastal toehold. The poem was "The Burial of Sir John Moore." Even then I could recognize the first two lines, and the last of that favorite of my boyhood. The first two lines are:

Not a drum was heard, not a funeral note,
As his corse to the rampart we hurried

I remembered that "hurried" rhymes with "buried." I recognized the rest of the poem, but later could remember only the last line, which comes after the hero has been left as the English sail away:

And left him alone in his glory.

Later, after a long search, I found a text. This, of course, would be in a forgotten and dilapidated copy of *The Home Book of Verse,* edition of 1912—a book that had never belonged to my father, God knows to whom. The author of the poem is a certain Charles Wolfe, a poet of no fame who died around 1820. It was one of the poems, I remember, which I had made my father read to me over and over, but not from that book.

Some time after the Mexican trip Eleanor went with me on a visit to meet my father and brother. On a Sunday afternoon, at my brother's house, I stood with a group of his friends, ice tinkling in glasses. I could see into another room where Eleanor and my father sat with chairs drawn almost together, heads leaning a little forward in a close and uninterrupted conversation.

By that time my father had announced to my brother that he himself had already made arrangements to go to a "retirement home" in Clarksville, where he would have a little apartment with a sitting room. The home was in a quiet section, where he could take walks.

On a later visit which Eleanor and I made to Kentucky my father was to come from Clarksville to my brother's house to see, and hold, our new baby daughter: a baby who so many years later would be thumbing over and over his old lexicon of Liddell and Scott. Of that afternoon of her babyhood I remember little beyond the fact that he held her, his face leaning slightly over her.

That was all I seemed to remember for some years except one fact of great clarity: a day or two later, as I backed our car out of the driveway of the retirement home I saw his face looking out at us. He had drawn the curtains apart at the window of his sitting room and was watching us go.

We went off through the streets of Clarksville. The town had long since become a booming little city. We went off through streets largely unfamiliar to me so long after the time when I had spent a year at school there. We drove on past factories and other signs of progress, down the buzzing and humming concrete slab to the point we joined the great highway northward.

That visit to Clarksville, then the face at a window, was the last time I was to see my father. Alive and conscious.

One night a year or so later I woke to the telephone by my bed. My father was dying. I managed to get a flight, and next morning at my arrival, he was still alive. He had collapsed the evening before while writing a letter and had fallen from his chair, unconscious. Later, when he became conscious, injections had relieved obviously intense pain. Now, unconscious, he occasionally moved. Once, as though by remarkable effort, his right arm slowly rose in the air, and the hand moved as though trying to grasp something.

My sister drove her fingernails into the biceps of my right arm until the tips seemed to be touching in the muscle. She said: "The medicine just drives the pain deeper."

After death had been certified, I went into his sitting room. The unfinished letter was still on the desk. Across the sheet, to the edge, was a long pen-stroke from the last word written, downward—apparently made as he fainted and fell. The pen was on the floor. I picked it up. I looked at the scarcely begun letter. It began: "Dear Son."

He was approaching his eighty-sixth birthday. He had willed to die alone, and without any medical intervention. The doctor discovered that it was cancer of the prostate. My father, as I have earlier said, had never in his life seen a doctor or spent a day in bed except during a long illness when he was forty-two years old. This was simply independence of spirit.

Katherine Anne Porter, my dear old friend, wrote me a letter from Liège, Belgium, dated February 4, 1955. I quote a passage with some indicated deletions:

The thought of your father suffering by himself because he didn't want to be trouble to any one is very painful; and must be to you. It was very heroic and characteristic, maybe he did what he wished to do, it takes very pure courage, surely above all at that age, to know death is near, and not ask any one to know what is happening. . . . I love his toughness of spirit, but he shouldn't have expected *you* to be tough about him! . . . I am sure everything was clear and right in his mind, but I understand the nature of loneliness.

1 / AFTER NIGHT FLIGHT SON REACHES BEDSIDE
OF ALREADY UNCONSCIOUS FATHER, WHOSE
RIGHT HAND LIFTS IN A SPASMODIC GESTURE,
AS THOUGH TRYING TO MAKE CONTACT: 1955

In Time's concatenation and
Carnal conventicle, I,
Arriving, being flung through dark and
The abstract flight-grid of sky,
Saw rising from the sweated sheet and
Ruck of bedclothes ritualistically
Reordered by the paid hand
Of mercy—saw rising the hand—

Christ, start again! What was it I,
Standing there, travel-shaken, saw
Rising? What could it be that I,
Caught sudden in gut- or conscience-gnaw,
Saw rising out of the past, which I
Saw now as twisted bedclothes? Like law,
The hand rose cold from History
To claw at a star in the black sky,

But could not reach that far—oh, cannot!
And the star horribly burned, burns,
For in darkness the wax-white clutch could not
Reach it, and white hand on wrist-stem turns,
Lifts in last tension of tendon, but cannot
Make contact—*oh, oop-si-daisy,* churns
The sad heart, *oh, atta-boy, daddio's got*
One more shot in the locker, peas-porridge hot—

But no. Like an eyelid the hand sank, strove
Downward, and in that darkening roar,
All things—all joy and the hope that strove,
The failed exam, the admired endeavor,
Prizes and prinkings, and the truth that strove,
And back of the capitol, boyhood's first whore—
Were snatched from me, and I could not move,
Naked in that black blast of his love.

Mother dead, land lost, stepmother haggard with kids,
Big Brother skedaddling off to Mexico
To make his fortune, gold or cattle or cards,
What could he do but what we see him doing?
Cutting crossties for the first railroad in the region,
Sixteen and strong as a man—was a man, by God!—
And the double-bit bit into red oak, and in that rhythm,
In his head, all day, marched the Greek paradigm:
That was all that was his, and all he could carry all day with him.

Λέγω, λέγεις, λέγει, and the axe swung.
That was that year, and the next year we see him
Revolve in his dream between the piece goods and cheese,
In a crossroads store, between peppermint candy and plow-points,
While the eaves drip, and beyond the black trees of winter
Last light grays out, and in the ruts of the lane

Water gleams, sober as steel. That was that land,
And that was the life, and he reached out and
Took the dime from the gray-scaled palm of the Negro plowhand's hand.

'Εν ἀρχῇ ἦν ὁ λόγος: in the beginning
Was the word, but in the end was
What? At the mirror, lather on chin, with a razor
Big as a corn-knife, or, so to the boy it seemed,
He stood, and said: 'Εν ἀρχῇ ἦν ὁ λόγος:
And laughed. And said: "That's Greek, now you know how it sounds!"
And laughed, and waved the bright blade like a toy.
And laughing from the deep of a dark conquest and joy,
Said: "Greek—but it wasn't for me. Let's get to breakfast, boy."

Years later, I find the old grammar, yellowed. Night
Is falling. Ash flakes from the log. The log
Glows, winks, wanes. Westward, the sky,
In one small area redeemed from gray, bleeds dully.
Beyond my window, athwart that red west,
The spruce bough, though snow-burdened, looks black,
Not white. The world lives by the trick of the eye, the trick
Of the heart. I hold the book in my hand, but God
—In what mercy, if mercy?—will not let me weep. But I
Do not want to weep. I want to understand.

Oh, let me understand what is that sound,
Like wind, that fills the enormous dark of my head.
Beyond my head there is no wind, the room
Darkening, the world beyond the room darkening,
And no wind beyond to cleave, unclot, the thickening
Darkness. There must be a way to state the problem.

The statement of a problem, no doubt, determines solution.
If once, clear and distinct, I could state it, then God
Could no longer fall back on His old alibi of ignorance.
I hear now my small son laugh from a farther room.

I know he sits there and laughs among his toys,
Teddy bear, letter blocks, yellow dumptruck, derrick, choo-choo—
Bright images, all, of Life's significance.
So I put the Greek grammar on the shelf, beside my own,
Unopened these thirty years, and leave the dark room,
And know that all night, while the constellations grind,
Beings with folded wings brood above that shelf,
Awe-struck and imbecile, and in the dark,
Amid History's vice and velleity, that poor book burns
Like fox-fire in the black swamp of the world's error.

In the turpitude of Time,
Hope dances on the razor edge.
I see those ever healing feet
Tread the honed edge above despair.
I see the song-wet lip and tossing hair.

The leaf unfolds the autumn weather.
The heart spills the horizon's light.
In the woods, the hunter, weeping, kneels,
And the dappled fawn weeps in contrition
For its own beauty. I hear the toad's intercession

For us, and all, who do not know
How cause flows backward from effect
To bless the past occasion, and
How Time's tongue lifts only to tell,
Minute by minute, what truth the brave heart will fulfill.

Can we—oh, could we only—believe
What annelid and osprey know,
And the stone, night-long, groans to divulge?
If we only could, then that star
That dawnward slants might sing to our human ear,

And joy, in daylight, run like feet,
And strength, in darkness, wait like hands,
And between the stone and the wind's voice
A silence wait to become our own song:
In the heart's last kingdom only the old are young.

Out of the woods where pollen is a powder of gold
Shaken from pistil of oak minutely, and of maple,
And is falling, and the tulip tree lifts, not yet tarnished,
The last calyx, in which chartreuse coolness recessed, dew,
Only this morning, lingered till noon—look,
Out of the woods, barefoot, the boy comes. He stands,
Hieratic, complete, in patched britches and that idleness of boyhood
Which asks nothing and is its own fulfilment:
In his hand a wand of peeled willow, boy-idle and aimless.

Poised between woods and the pasture, sun-green and green shadow,
Hair sweat-dark, brow bearing a smudge of gold pollen, lips
Parted in some near-smile of boyhood bemusement,
Dangling the willow, he stands, and I—I stare
Down the tube and darkening corridor of Time
That breaks, like tears, upon that sunlit space,
And staring, I know who he is, and would cry out.
Out of my knowledge, I would cry out and say:
Listen! Say: *Listen! I know—oh, I know—let me tell you!*

That scene is in Trigg County, and I see it.
Trigg County is in Kentucky, and I have been there,
But never remember the spring there. I remember
A land of cedar-shade, blue, and the purl of limewater,
But the pasture parched, and the voice of the lost joree
Unrelenting as conscience, and sick, and the afternoon throbs,
And the sun's hot eye on the dry leaf shrivels the aphid,
And the sun's heel does violence in the corn-balk.
That is what I remember, and so the scene

I had seen just now in the mind's eye, vernal,
Is altered, and I strive to cry across the dry pasture,
But cannot, nor move, for my feet, like dry corn-roots, cleave
Into the hard earth, and my tongue makes only the dry,
Slight sound of wind on the autumn corn-blade. The boy,
With imperial calm, crosses a space, rejoins
The shadow of woods, but pauses, turns, grins once,
And is gone. And one high oak leaf stirs gray, and the air,
Stirring, freshens to the far favor of rain.

This book is printed on acid-free paper meeting
the requirements of the American National Standard
for Permanence of Paper for Printed Library Materials.
∞

Library of Congress Cataloging-in-Publication Data

Warren, Robert Penn, 1905-
   Portrait of a father / Robert Penn Warren.
     p.   cm.
   ISBN 0-8131-1655-4
   1. Warren, Robert Penn, 1905-   —Biography—Family. 2. Warren,
Robert Franklin. 3. Warren family. 4. Fathers—United States—
Biography. 5. Authors, American—20th century—Biography.
I. Title.
PS3545.A748Z477   1988
813' .52—dc19
[B]   88-5